Isaac Collins, John S. Powell

# A List of some of the Benevolent Institutions of the City of Philadelphia and Their Legal Titles

Anatiposi

Isaac Collins, John S. Powell

# A List of some of the Benevolent Institutions of the City of Philadelphia and Their Legal Titles

Reprint of the original.

1st Edition 2023  |  ISBN: 978-3-38230-134-7

Anatiposi Verlag is an imprint of Outlook Verlagsgesellschaft mbH.

Verlag (Publisher): Outlook Verlag GmbH, Zeilweg 44, 60439 Frankfurt, Deutschland
Vertretungsberechtigt (Authorized to represent): E. Roepke, Zeilweg 44, 60439 Frankfurt, Deutschland
Druck (Print): Books on Demand GmbH, In de Tarpen 42, 22848 Norderstedt, Deutschland

# A LIST

OF SOME OF THE

# BENEVOLENT INSTITUTIONS

OF THE

## CITY OF PHILADELPHIA.

AND

## THEIR LEGAL TITLES.

# A LIST

OF SOME OF THE

## BENEVOLENT INSTITUTIONS

OF THE

# CITY OF PHILADELPHIA,

AND THEIR

## LEGAL TITLES,

TOGETHER WITH

## A FORM OF DEVISE AND BEQUEST TO THEM.

COMPILED BY

ISAAC COLLINS

JOHN S. POWELL,

ATTORNEY AT LAW.

PHILADELPHIA:
HENRY B. ASHMEAD, BOOK AND JOB PRINTER,
SANSOM STREET ABOVE ELEVENTH.
1859.

# CERTIFICATE.

*The undersigned have carefully examined the Legal Titles of the* BENEVOLENT INSTITUTIONS *in this pamphlet, and believe them to be correct.*

ELI K. PRICE,
N. B. BROWNE.

PHILADELPHIA, MARCH 1859.

# NOTICE.

*Two thousand copies of this pamphlet have been printed, of which it is intended to send a few copies to each of the benevolent institutions mentioned therein, also a copy to members of the bar and to conveyancers, and to about one thousand five hundred of our wealthy citizens, and if the requisite funds are provided, to have the pamphlet stereotyped, in order that small editions of five hundred copies, may from time to time be printed and put into circulation.*

MARCH 30, 1859.

*The following* FORMS OF BEQUEST OR DEVISE *will, by insert-ing in the blank space the Title of the Institution, intend-ed to be designated by the will, answer for all* INCORPORATED INSTITUTIONS.

## OF PERSONAL PROPERTY.

I do give and bequeath to the           at Philadelphia, the sum of

---

## OF REAL ESTATE.

I do give and devise unto the         at Philadelphia, their successors and assigns forever, all that cer-tain, (describe the real estate,) with the appurtenances.

Persons intending to bequeath or devise to Charitable In-stitutions *not incorporated,* are advised to consult counsel as to the legal form.

---

Attention must be given to the following important law, viz:

---

Extract from an Act of Assembly, approved 26th April, 1855, relative to Devises and Bequests to Charitable Institutions.

"SECTION 11. No estate, real or personal, shall hereafter be bequeathed, devised or conveyed to any body politic, or to any person, *in trust for religious or charitable uses,* except the same be done by deed or will, attested by two credible, and at the time disinterested witnesses, *at least one calendar month before the decease of the testator or alienor;* and all dispositions of property contrary hereto, shall be void and go to the *residuary* legatee or devisee, next of kin or heirs according to law; *Pro-vided,* That any disposition of property within said period, *bona fide* made for a fair valuable consideration, shall not be hereby avoided."

# INTRODUCTION.

---

THE object of this publication is to furnish an accurate list of the Charitable Associations of our city, and the usual and proper forms of bequest or devise, for the convenience of those who may wish to remember them in their *Wills*, or in conveyance of property in anticipation of death.

It is believed to contain a full and accurate list of all such charities of a public character, but is not intended to include private beneficial associations, or those of a sectarian nature.

If it shall prove serviceable in directing the course of liberality, in a single instance, to any one of our many noble and worthy objects of public and private benevolence, the aim of the compilers will be fully attained.

NOTE.—A conspicuous color has been selected for the cover, so that this pamphlet may be readily distinguished from any other.

# THE HOWARD INSTITUTION, UNDER THE CARE OF AN ASSOCIATION OF WOMEN FRIENDS OF PHILADELPHIA.

*Incorporated by the Court of Common Pleas, September 20, 1858.*

Situated at No. 1612 Poplar Street.

*President*, Rebecca Collins.                    *Secretary*, Rebecca T. Haines.
*Treasurer*, Regina S. Kimber.

This Charitable Institution was opened for a home for discharged Female Prisoners, of rather superior minds and some education, who *have not been prostitutes;* as the Magdalen Asylum and the Rosine offer a home for the latter class. "*The Association of Women Friends*," who, for thirty years past, have made weekly visits to our prisons, state, as of frequent occurrence, that female prisoners often afford satisfactory evidence of sincere repentance, and earnest desires to reform and regain their lost characters; yet, when discharged from prison, they are, for want of employment, often reduced to great distress, and of course are subjected to sore temptations. *To starve or steal seems to be the alternative left for them.* Men can obtain employment; but what family will receive and employ women just discharged from prison, and without any character? But such are received into this asylum, and are industriously employed, until the sincerity of their desires to reform have been *fully tested;* after which, suitable places, *far in the country,* are provided, and they are thus removed from the corrupting influence of former associates. Many such have been saved; but for want of more funds the usefulness of *The Howard Institution* is greatly circumscribed. Having no funds invested, it is entirely dependent on donations and annual subscriptions.

## THE CONTRIBUTORS TO THE PENNSYLVANIA HOSPITAL.

### *Incorporated* 1751.

Pine between 8th and 9th Streets.

*President,* Mordecai L. Dawson.                    *Secretary,* William Biddle.
*Treasurer,* John T. Lewis.

Connected with this great public charity, and under the direction of the same Board of Managers, is an extensive Hospital for insane males, and another for insane females in the Twenty-fourth Ward, extending from Market Street to the Haverford Road.

## THE HOSPITAL OF THE PROTESTANT EPISCOPAL CHURCH IN PHILADELPHIA.

### *Charter of Incorporation granted July 18th,* 1851.

Cor. Huntingdon and Front Streets, Kensington.   Office, 524 Walnut St.

*President,* Right Rev. Alonzo Potter.            *Secretary,* Rev. J. A. Childs.
*Treasurer,* George L. Harrison.

Admits patients of every denomination, color and country.

## CHARITY HOSPITAL.

### *Incorporated* 1859.

Buttonwood below Broad Street.

*President,* Hon. Oswald Thompson.                *Secretary,* Burrough Price.
*Treasurer,* John Sharp.

*Board of Trustees.*—Hon. Oswald Thompson, Hon. James R. Ludlow, George Nugent, Esq., Robert Morris, Esq., Rev. A. A. Willits, Rev. Kingston Goddard, Rev. W. O. Prentiss, Rev. Alfred Cookman, Hon. Wm. D. Kelly.

Established for the benefit of all citizens and strangers who require and seek its aid.

# WILLS' HOSPITAL FOR THE DISEASES OF THE BLIND AND LAME.

### *It is not Incorporated.*

Situated between 18th and 19th Streets, opposite Logan Square.

*President*, John Rodman Paul.               *Secretary*, Edward Hopper.

The Wills' Hospital for the Diseases of the Eye and Limb was founded by the late James Wills, of Philadelphia, who bequeathed to the Mayor and Corporation of the City a part of his estate for that purpose.

It is beautifully situated on Race Street, between Eighteenth and Nineteenth Streets, immediately opposite to Logan Square; and was opened for the reception of patients in 1834—admission being granted to such only as are capable either of cure or relief.

A Board of Managers, appointed by the Councils, confide the medical charge of the Hospital to four Surgeons, who attend in turn, and give their services gratuitously.

The smallness of the funds remaining after the purchase of the lot and the erection of the building has not allowed the admission at any one time of more than thirty-five or forty persons; but the usefulness of the Institution has been greatly extended by the appropriation of certain days in every week for advice to out-patients, who flock to it from all parts of the city and country, in number annually from 1500 to 2000.

The same reason has restricted its operations chiefly to the Diseases of the Eye; though, with greater means, more ample accommodations could be provided for the Lame also, and thus afford to the city the advantages almost of another general hospital.

*Form of a Legacy.*—I give and bequeath to the City of Philadelphia, in trust, for the use of the Wills' Hospital for the relief of the indigent blind and the lame, the sum of                    dollars.

---

# THE SAINT JOSEPH'S HOSPITAL.

### *Incorporated* 1850.

Girard Avenue between 16th and 17th Streets.

*President*, Rt. Rev. James T. Wood.          *Secretary*, James A. Doyle.
*Treasurer*, Charles A. Repplier.

Under the control of the Roman Catholic Church, but admits persons of every creed, color and country.

# THE CHILDREN'S HOSPITAL OF PHILADELPHIA.

*Incorporated* 1859.

Blight Street, east of Broad Street, and between Pine and Lombard Street.

*President*, Mordecai D. Lewis.                    *Secretary*, John H. Atwood.
*Treasurer*, Morton P. Henry.

Intended for sick children of Poor Parents, between the ages of two and twelve years.

---

# THE FEMALE MEDICAL COLLEGE OF PENNSYLVANIA.

*Incorporated March* 11, 1850.

No. 628 Arch Street.

*President*, Charles D. Cleveland.                    *Secretary*, William S. Pierce.
*Treasurer*, Marmaduke Moore.

Designed to give to women as thorough a medical education as can be obtained by men; so that they can skilfully and successfully administer to that large class of diseases peculiar to her sex, and be the *intelligent* as well as the sympathizing attendant in the chambers of the sick.

---

# HOWARD HOSPITAL AND INFIRMARY OF IN-CURABLES.

*Incorporated May*, 1854.

Situated between Christian and Carpenter and 15th and 16th Streets.

*President*, Jesper Harding.                    *Secretary*, E. McClelland.
*Treasurer*, John McClure.

Established for the gratuitous relief of the poor.

# THE UNION SCHOOL AND CHILDREN'S HOME.

*Incorporated April, 1851.*

Corner of 12th and Fitzwater Streets.

*President*, Mrs. Joel Jones.                    *Secretary*, Mrs. J. C. Pechin.
                    *Treasurer*, Mrs. T. R. Maris.

TRUSTEES.—*President*, George H. Stuart.          *Secretary*, John C. Pechin.

The object of this Institution, (the first of its kind in Philadelphia,) is to prevent pauperism and crime, and to promote industry and increase laborers, by removing children, under thirteen years of age, from the evil influences of the city to the healthful and moral atmosphere of the country during their minority.

---

# THE NORTHERN HOME FOR FRIENDLESS CHILDREN.

*Incorporated January 26, 1854.*

Corner of 23d and Brown Streets.

*President*, Mrs. E. W. Hutter.                    *Secretary*, Mrs. A. V. Murphey.
                    *Treasurer*, Mrs. R. Hammett.

TRUSTEES.—*President*, Thomas Earp.          *Secretary*, MacGregor J. Mitcheson.
                    *Treasurer*, John W. Clagborn.

For the support and tuition of deserted or friendless children under 12 years of age, with power to provide them with suitable homes, until their majority, and similar in other respects to the above institution.

## THE HOUSE OF REFUGE.
### *Incorporated March 23rd, 1826.*

Situated between Parrish and Poplar and 22d and 24th Streets.

*President*, Thomas Earp.                    *Secretary*, Alexander Henry.
*Treasurer*, George W. Fobes.

This is a school for the education and moral improvement of Juvenile Delinquents, and will accommodate in the White Department, four hundred and thirty-two, and in the Colored Department, one hundred and eighty, in all six hundred and twelve children. This Institution is so well known, and its importance and extensive usefulness has been so frequently acknowledged by an expression of public sentiment, that any additional notice of it seems to be unnecessary.

---

## THE WESTERN PROVIDENT SOCIETY AND CHILDREN'S HOME OF PHILADELPHIA.
### *Incorporated April 8, 1858.*

At present on Market above Park Street, 24th Ward. Intend to build at S. E. corner of Logan and Venango Street, Twenty fourth Ward.

MANAGERS.—*President*, Mrs. Franklin Bacon.     *Secretary*, Miss E. P. Eakin.
*Treasurer*, Mrs. Samuel Field.

TRUSTEES.—*President*, Nathaniel B. Browne.     *Secretary*, Constant M. Eakin.

Similar to the Northern Home for Friendless Children in design, character and chartered privileges.

---

## UNION TEMPORARY HOME FOR CHILDREN.
### *Incorporated February, 1857.*

House located at the N. E. corner of 16th and Poplar Streets.

*President*, Miss Susan J. O'Neill.          *Secretary*, Mrs. Charles Brown.
COUNCIL—*President*, Richard Vaux.          *Secretary*, D. C. M'Cammon.
*Treasurer*, E. W. Clark.

This institution is somewhat similar to the Northern Home for Friendless Children except that in some cases a small weekly sum is received from the parents, and the children received are generally younger.

# FOSTER HOME ASSOCIATION OF PHILADELPHIA.

*Chartered by the Governor January* 14, 1839.

Situated between 20th and 21st and Hamilton and Spring Garden Streets.

*First Directress*, Mrs. G. W. Toland.          *Secretary*, —— ——
Treasurer, Mrs. E. S. Simmons.
Council—E. K. Price, John Welsh.

This Institution is for the reception of children of widows and widowers, who pay according to their ability, not exceeding 75 cents per week. A limited number of children are supported entirely by the Association, when long-continued illness of the parent or other causes throw them upon its charity. The children are received from three to nine years of age, and retained until suitable places are obtained for them, or their surviving parent receives them.

---

# THE TEMPORARY HOME ASSOCIATION OF PHILADELPHIA.

*Incorporated January* 29, 1852.

No. 37 Zane Street.

*President*, Sidney Ann Lewis.          *Secretary*, S. F. Dawes.
Treasurer, Mary W. Brooks.

This charity is intended to furnish a cheap and comfortable place of boarding to single women and children until they can procure employment.

# THE NEWS BOYS' AID SOCIETY OF PHILADELPHIA.

*Incorporated June 7, 1858.*

No. 221 Spruce Street.

*President*, John Bohlen.                                    *Secretary*, George S. Fox.

*Treasurer*, William Purves.

The objects of this Society are to provide lodging and education for homeless and indigent boys engaged in the occupation of vending newspapers and periodicals, in the City of Philadelphia, and to encourage in them, by suitable means, habits of morality and economy.

---

## PHILADELPHIA LYING IN CHARITY FOR ATTENDING INDIGENT WOMEN AT THEIR OWN HOMES,

*Incorporated May 7, 1832.*

AND

### THE PHILADELPHIA NURSE SOCIETY,

NOW UNITED AND KNOWN AS

## THE PHILADELPHIA LYING IN CHARITY AND NURSE SOCIETY.

No. 931 Race Street.

*President*, Casper Wistar, M. D.                          *Secretary*, Isaac S. Williams.

*Treasurer*, Edward Parrish.

The objects of this charity are to afford medical aid to indigent married women at their own homes during their confinement, to provide nourishment adapted to their condition during their convalescence, and to furnish to such as require it a competent nurse. Incidentally to these objects, attention is given to the careful training of suitable women for the responsible duties of the lying-in chamber, and a register of qualified nurses is kept at the Nurses' Home for public reference. This charity is entirely dependent on donations and annual subscriptions, of which more is requisite for its support.

## THE PRESTON RETREAT.

*Incorporated, by Act of Assembly, June 16, 1836.*

Situated between 20th and 21st and Hamilton and Spring Garden Streets.

*President,* John M. Ogden.                    *Secretary,* Edward Hopper.
*Treasurer,* Eli K. Price.

The late Dr. Preston, by his will, bequeathed funds to establish an institution for a lying in charity, which it is intended soon to open.

---

## UNION BENEVOLENT ASSOCIATION.

*Incorporated March 28, 1837.*

Office, South 7th, two doors North of Sansom Street.

*President,* Charles S. Wurts.                    *Secretary,* John H. Atwood.
*Treasurer,* Edmund Wilcox.

This charitable Institution is so extensively known and approved of, that it is unnecessary to state more than the legal title. It is obliged to rely upon the subscriptions and donations of the citizens for its annual expenditures, which from the great extent of its benevolent operations are necessarily very large.

# THE PROVIDENT SOCIETY FOR EMPLOYING THE POOR.

*Incorporated,* 1842.

Prune below Sixth Street.

*President,* John A. Brown.　　　　　　*Secretary,* William H. Larned.

*Treasurer,* William L. Edwards.

This Society was first organized as early as 1824, by Bishop White, Roberts Vaux, Alexander Henry, Thomas Astley, Philip Garrett and others, having for its object *not the distribution of alms,* but to *provide employment* in the winter season, when work is with difficulty obtained, principally to aged women, widows and mothers with young children, not however to the exclusion of other deserving persons. In the winter of 1856–7, 678 women were employed, who made 16,200 shirts.

---

# THE FEMALE SOCIETY OF PHILADELPHIA, FOR THE RELIEF AND EMPLOYMENT OF THE POOR.

*Incorporated January* 12, 1815.

No. 112 N. 7th Street.

*Clerk,* Julianna Randolph.　　　　　　*Treasurer,* Mary Ann Bacon.

This Society is the oldest of this character in the city, having been instituted in the autumn of the year 1793, following the yellow fever, which left many widows and orphans dependent and suffering. Its object is to furnish employment during the winter season, at the House of Industry, to aged women and those with young children, who cannot obtain other work. A nursery department, well warmed rooms and a comfortable dinner are provided, and a small daily compensation given. All that are employed are visited and kept under care, and their necessities attended to when sick. One hundred and fifty women and fifty children are now on the list. Some out-door relief is also furnished to aged persons who are unable to work.

## WESTERN ASSOCIATION OF LADIES, FOR THE RELIEF AND EMPLOYMENT OF THE POOR.

*Incorporated September* 15, 1856.

17th between Chestnut and Market Streets.

*President*, Sarah F. Key.  *Secretary*, H. A. Zell.

*Treasurer*, E. M. Morris.

The object of this association is to afford employment, for which a small compensation is given, to aged and infirm females and those who, having little children, are unable to leave them to go out to work. They are employed in the house, in a large and airy sewing room, while the little children are placed in the nursery, under the superintendence of competent nurses; and those who attend the public schools are allowed to come and partake of a comfortable dinner, which is freely given to all. The whole is under the charge of the lady managers, who are daily in attendance.

## THE NORTHERN ASSOCIATION OF THE CITY AND COUNTY OF PHILADELPHIA, FOR THE RELIEF AND EMPLOYMENT OF POOR WOMEN.

*Incorporated April,* 1849.

*President*, Lucretia Mott.  *Secretary*, Lydia Gillingham.

Many infirm and destitute women have, by this charity, been enabled to obtain a living, who would otherwise have been a burthen upon society.

## THE CENTRAL EMPLOYMENT ASSOCIATION.

*Incorporated.*

S. E. corner Ninth and Green Streets.

*President*, Abigal W. Ellis.  *Secretary*, Ann A. Townsend.

*Treasurer*, Elizabeth W. Lippincott.

The object of this Association is to give employment in sewing, at a reasonable compensation, to deserving poor women, the garments thus made being designed for gratuitous distribution among the adult sick and infirm, and to children.

## THE PHILADELPHIA SOCIETY FOR THE EMPLOYMENT AND INSTRUCTION OF THE POOR.

*Incorporated* 1858.

Catharine between 7th and 8th Streets.

*President*, Thomas T. Tasker.　　　　　*Secretary*, Coleman L. Nicholson.
*Treasurer*, Wistar Morris.

For the efficient promotion of its objects, the society erected the building known as " *The Moyamensing House of Industry*," on Catharine Street above Seventh. No age, color or sex is excluded from the benefits of the institution. To help the poor to help themselves, is the purpose kept in view. There are lodgings for about one hundred and fifty persons; and twice this number are not unfrequently furnished with meals in a single day. There are two work rooms, which in the winter season are well filled with women employed in sewing. Baths and conveniences for washing both their persons and clothing are furnished the poor, free of charge. Clothing and nourishment are given to the sick, and fuel is sold in small quantities at about half the cost. Efforts are made to procure employment for inmates whose characters prove satisfactory. An industrial school for girls, an infant school, and a school for colored children are maintained with an aggregate average attendance exceeding two hundred. *A Dispensary is sustained, with a resident apothecary*. A physician attends daily to prescribe, and out door cases are attended by four visiting physicians. With the exception of an income of less than $100, the society is wholly dependent for support upon annual subscriptions. 　·

---

## THE PENNSYLVANIA INSTITUTION FOR THE DEAF AND DUMB.

*Incorporated February*, 1821.

Corner of Broad and Pine Streets.

*President*, Franklin Bache.　　　　　*Secretary*, James J. Barclay.
*Treasurer*, John Bacon.

Indigent deaf mutes are received, between the ages of ten and twenty years of age, from all parts of Pennsylvania.

# THE PENNSYLVANIA INSTITUTION FOR THE INSTRUCTION OF THE BLIND.

*Incorporated January 27, 1834.*

Corner of Race and 20th Streets.

*President*, Samuel Breck.        *Secretary*, Theodore Cuyler.
*Treasurer*, Robert Patterson.

---

# THE CONTRIBUTORS TO THE ASYLUM FOR THE RELIEF OF PERSONS DEPRIVED OF THE USE OF THEIR REASON.

*Not incorporated.*

Near Frankford, 23rd Ward.

*Clerk*, William Bettle.        *Treasurer*, Horatio C. Wood.

This Asylum is in a pleasant and healthy situation in one of the rural districts of the City of Philadelphia. It was founded in the year 1813, by members of the Society of Friends, with a view of affording to those afflicted with insanity the domestic comforts usually found in a private family, combined with skilful moral and medical treatment.

### FORMS OF LEGACY.

#### I. FORM OF A BEQUEST OF PERSONAL ESTATE.

"I give and bequeath to A. B. and C. D., and the survivor of them, and the executors and administrators of such survivor, the sum of
in trust for the use of an Institution in Philadelphia, known by the name of 'The Contributors to the Asylum for the Relief of Persons deprived of the Use of their Reason,' and to be paid by the said Trustees to the Treasurer for the time being of the said Institution."

#### II. FORM OF A DEVISE OF REAL ESTATE.

"I give and devise to A. B. and C. D., and their heirs, all that (here describe the property)    together with the appurtenances, to hold to them, the said A. B. and C. D., and the survivor of them, and the heirs of such survivor forever; in trust nevertheless, for the sole use and benefit of an Institution in Philadelphia, known by the name of 'The Contributors to the Asylum for the Relief of Persons Deprived of the Use of their Reason,' and upon this further trust, absolutely to dispose of, and convey the same, either in fee, or for such other estate, and in such way and manner, as the Contributors to the said Asylum shall, at any meeting or meetings, order, direct and appoint."

2

## THE PENNSYLVANIA TRAINING SCHOOL FOR FEEBLE-MINDED CHILDREN.

*Incorporated April 7, 1853.—Amended by Court of Common Pleas, February 20th, 1858.*

*President,* Rt. Rev. Alonzo Potter.  *Secretary,* Franklin Taylor.
*Treasurer,* Alexander Fullerton.

This Institution is doing a good work to a most needy class of children, and could do much more with increased means. Its claims upon the *benevolent, for support and endowment,* are in proportion to the helplessness and need of those for whose benefit it is designed, and it is most earnestly recommended to their favorable consideration. It is at present located at Germantown, but soon will be removed to Media, Delaware Co., Pa., where new buildings are being erected, which will accommodate one hundred and thirty children.

## THE ORPHANS' SOCIETY OF PHILADELPHIA.

*Incorporated January 29, 1816.*

Corner of Cherry and 18th Streets.

*Directress,* Sarah W. Fisher.  *Secretary,* Rebecca Gratz
*Treasurer,* Mrs. Henry J. Williams.

## PHILADELPHIA ASSOCIATION FOR THE RELIEF OF DISABLED FIREMEN.

*Incorporated March 25, 1835.*

*President,* George W. Tryon.  *Secretary,* William T. Butler.
*Treasurer,* Jacob Esher.

The object of this Association is the Relief of Disabled Firemen, their widows and orphans, and the relief of persons, *not firemen,* who may sustain personal injury by fire apparatus.

# INDIGENT WIDOWS' AND SINGLE WOMEN'S SO-CIETY OF PHILADELPHIA.

### *Incorporated* 1819.

Cherry Street near 18th.

*Directress*, Mrs. H. L. Hodge.        *Secretary*, Mrs. J. K. Kane.
*Treasurer*, Mrs. I. C. Jones, Jr.

Is intended to furnish a comfortable home for indigent and aged women who have known better days.

---

# PENN ASYLUM FOR INDIGENT WIDOWS AND SIN-GLE WOMEN OF THE CITY OF PHILADELPHIA.

### *Incorporated December* 6, 1852.

Corner of West and Wood Streets, Kensington.

*President*, Emeline Claridge.        *Secretary*, Mary Wattles.
*Treasurer*, Elizabeth Carr.

Object same as preceding charity.

---

# THE GRANDOM INSTITUTION.

### *Incorporated, by Act of Assembly, April* 23, 1841.

Office, No. 811 Arch Street.

*President*, John M. Ogden.        *Secretary and Treasurer*, Henry C. Townsend.

The object of the Grandom Institution is two fold; the income of part of the fund is loaned to young men on satisfactory security, to commence the various pursuits which they have learned, the income of the other fund is employed in furnishing coal to the deserving poor, but not the intemperate, at a reduced price, about one half of the cost.

## THE APPRENTICES' LIBRARY COMPANY OF PHILADELPHIA.

### *Incorporated, A. D.* 1820.

Corner of 5th and Arch Streets.

*President*, James J. Barclay. *Secretary*, Thomas Ridgway.
*Treasurer*, Samuel Mason.

A library for the free use of minors of both sexes, and contained in 1858, about 15,000 volumes.

---

## THE YOUNG MEN'S INSTITUTE.

### *Incorporated May* 21*st*, 1851.

Has no building appropriated to its use.

*President*, William Welsh. *Secretary*, William L. Rehn.
*Treasurer*, S. Morris Waln.

The objects of this institution are " to encourage and foster among the young men of our laboring population in the city and county of Philadelphia, the spirit of self-improvement, by the establishment of libraries, reading-rooms, lectures, &c." To carry out these objects, the Board of Trustees, from a fund of about $31,000 entrusted to them, loaned to the five following co-operating institutions each $5,000 without interest, reserving about $6,000 for a fund, the income from which is expended to promote the objects of the institution. The five institutions referred to are as follows:

## THE SPRING GARDEN INSTITUTE.

*Incorporated by Act of Assembly 1851—Charter amended by Court of Common Pleas, December 1, 1856.*

N. E. corner of Broad and Spring Garden Streets.

*President,* John M. Ogden.                    *Secretary,* John W. Dixon.
*Treasurer,* Charles B. Trego.

This Institution has a library and reading room, and ample accommodations for the delivery of lectures, and also class-rooms.

---

## THE MECHANIC'S INSTITUTE OF SOUTHWARK.

*Incorporated June 14, 1852.*

*President,* H. A. Gildea.                    *Secretary,* E. C. Bonsall, Jr.
*Treasurer,* William Steadman.

Fifth Street below Washington Avenue.

Same as above.

---

## THE MOYAMENSING LITERARY INSTITUTE.

*Not incorporated.*

S. E. corner of 11th and Catharine Streets.

*President,* John U. Giller.                    *Secretary,* William J. Ramage.
*Treasurer,* William J. Reed.

Same as above.

# THE PHILADELPHIA CITY INSTITUTE.

## *Incorporated June 8, 1852.*

*President,* William H. French.  *Secretary,* P. C. Houton.
*Treasurer,* William Rhoads.

Corner of 18th and Chestnut Streets.

Same object as preceding.

---

# THE WEST PHILADELPHIA INSTITUTE.

## *Incorporated February 2, 1853.*

William, North of Market Street.

*President,* James Miller.  *Secretary,* J. W. Van Houton, Jr.
*Treasurer,* James Allen.

Same object as preceding.

---

# THE TRUSTEES OF WAGNER FREE INSTITUTE OF SCIENCE.

Second Story of "SPRING GARDEN HALL," Corner of Thirteenth and Spring Garden Streets.

## *Incorporated March 9, 1855.*

*President,* William Wagner.  *Secretary,* George Inman Riche.

This Institute is free to persons of both sexes, and the room can seat four hundred to five hundred persons.

SCHEDULE OF PROPERTY DONATED TO THE WAGNER FREE INSTITUTE OF SCIENCE, BY PROF. WM. WAGNER.

250,000 specimens of Minerals, collected from all parts of the inhabitable earth. This collection covers the whole field of Mineralogy; and is, perhaps, with one exception, the most valuable in the United States.

250,000 specimens of Geologic and Organic Remains, of rare value to the student, illustrating, as they do, the various races which are known to have flourished in the earlier geological periods.

200,000 specimens of recent Shells, for the purpose of comparison with their extinct *genera,* found in the various strata of the earth's crust.

25,000 specimens of Dried Plants, constituting an extensive and valuable Herbarium for botanical illustration,

A large and well arranged series of Diagrams, illustrative of various topics in Natural History, and of geological phenomena.

Professor Wagner's Library, Philosophical Apparatus, Maps, and Cabinet Cases.

# PENNSYLVANIA INSTITUTE FOR THE ENCOURAGEMENT OF APPRENTICES AND AMATEURS IN THE WORKS OF INGENUITY AND DESIGN.

*Incorporated 1856.*

Fallon's Building, No. 520 Walnut Street.

*President,* W. H. Allen, LL. D.  *Secretary,* Charles P. Perot.
*Treasurer,* Tobins M. Huber.

The object of this institute is to encourage, cultivate and promote the talents of those only at, and under, the age of twenty-five years, by means of a library of scientific and other works, explanatory lectures, cabinet of specimens, appertaining to scientific subjects, skill and talent, and such awards to the meritorious and ingenious as they may deserve.

---

# PHILADELPHIA SCHOOL OF DESIGN FOR WOMEN.

*Not Incorporated.*

No. 1334 Chestnut Street.

*President,* Joseph Harrison.  *Secretary and Treasurer,* P. P. Morris.

---

# INDUSTRIAL HOME FOR THE INSTRUCTION OF GIRLS IN THE ARTS OF HOUSEWIFERY AND SEWING.

*Not Incorporated.*

No. 321 South Thirteenth Street.

*President,* Mrs. J. C. Pechin.  *Secretary,* Mrs. M. E. Finley.
*Treasurer,* Miss E. W. Lewis.

Girls over twelve years of age are received and trained for service in private families.

# THE PHILADELPHIA SOCIETY FOR THE ESTABLISHMENT AND SUPPORT OF CHARITY SCHOOLS.

*Incorporated April 6, 1791.*

Walnut near 6th Street.

*President,* James J. Barclay.      *Secretary,* J. C. Turnpenny.

*Treasurer,* J. B. Ellison.

---

# INFANT SCHOOL SOCIETY OF PHILADELPHIA.

*Incorporated.*

*President,* Mrs. Samuel Moore, M. D.      *Secretary,* Miss C. A. Wiegand.

*Treasurer,* Miss E. Ewing.

---

# MAGDALEN SOCIETY OF PHILADELPHIA.

*Incorporated in 1802.*

Corner of 21st and Race Streets.

*President,* Rt. Rev. Alonzo Potter.      *Secretary,* Joshua W. Ash, M. D.

*Treasurer,* William Biddle.

The object is the reformation, employment and instruction of females who have led immoral lives, and there is reason to believe several hundred females have, through the instrumentality of this Society, been restored to the paths of virtue and happiness.

## THE ROSINE ASSOCIATION OF PHILADELPHIA.

*Incorporated April* 10, 1848.

8th above Wood Street.

*President*, Mary B. Thain.　　　　　　　　*Secretary*, Harriet Probasco.
*Treasurer*, Mira Townsend, 622 Race Street.

The *Rosine Association* of Philadelphia was *incorporated April* 11*th*, 1848, "to secure from vice and degradation a class of women who have forfeited their claims to the respect of the virtuous—to prepare and maintain for them an Asylum, which, by its system of religious instruction, shall elevate their moral nature—teach them how to gain an honest living by the 'work of their own hands,' and eventually to render them useful members of the community."

The members of this Society are females, but *every person* is invited to become a *contributor*.

The Institution is at present located at 320 North Eighth Street, in a private dwelling, where it will remain until funds can be obtained to erect a more suitable building.

The limited funds of the Association have prevented the managers from obtaining a building sufficiently large to admit the numerous applicants, many of whom cannot be received for want of room and suitable accommodations.

---

## FUEL SAVINGS SOCIETY OF THE CITY AND LIBERTIES OF PHILADELPHIA.

*Established*, 1821.　　　　　*Incorporated*, 1837.

*President*, Townsend Sharpless.　　　　*Treasurer*, Samuel J. Sharpless.
*Secretary*, Edward Speakman.

Its object is to encourage the poor to deposit small portions of their earnings during the summer, to be returned to them in coal during the winter at reduced prices.

## PHILADELPHIA DISPENSARY.

*Instituted April*, 12, 1786.

Fifth St., between Library and Walnut, opposite Independence Square.

*President*, William F. Griffitts.                    *Secretary*, Casper Wistar.
*Treasurer*, John M. Whitall.

Its object is gratuitous medical advice, surgical aid and medicines to the poor and necessitous.

---

## THE NORTHERN DISPENSARY OF PHILADELPHIA.

*Incorporated March* 26, 1817.—*Amended June* 4, 1855.

603 Spring Garden Street.

*President*, George W. Tryon.                    *Secretary*, John Kessler, Jr.
*Treasurer*, Joseph Warner.

As a proof of the usefulness of this Institution, the Managers would only refer to the Report for the year last past (1858), wherein it will be found that, (with their limited means,) they have extended relief to 9139 patients, being an increase of 2166 over any previous year.

---

## THE HOMŒOPATHIC MEDICAL COLLEGE OF PENN-SYLVANIA.

*Incorporated April* 8, 1848.

Filbert Street above 11th.

*President*, A. V. Parsons.                    *Secretary*, William A. Reed, M. D.
*Treasurer*, Henry Horner.

Number of graduates three hundred and thirty-four. To this institution there is attached a Dispensary, open every day, (Sunday excepted,) from 12 to 1 o'clock.

# PHILADELPHIA SOCIETY FOR ALLEVIATING THE MISERIES OF PUBLIC PRISONS.

*Instituted* 1797.—*Incorporated* 1833.

Office, corner of 7th and George Streets.

*President*, James J. Barclay.　　*Secretaries*, W. P. Foulke, E. Townsend.
*Treasurer*, H. C. Wood.

The objects of the Society are to visit prisoners while in jail, assist them with pecuniary aid, when deserving, on their discharge; to improve prison discipline and prison architecture, &c. A committee is appointed to visit the prisoners weekly, to give counsel and advice to the prisoners, and to procure situations for the deserving when discharged.

---

# PENNSYLVANIA BIBLE SOCIETY.

*Incorporated January* 30, 1810.—*Amended March* 7, 1840.

Corner 7th and Walnut Streets.

*President*, Rev. Albert Barnes.　　*Secretary*, Rev. Richard Newton.
*Treasurer*, John W. Claghorn.

This was the first Bible Society organized in the United States. It has been entrusted with legacies, which have been faithfully disbursed, by the distribution of the Holy Bible, without note or comment, among the destitute poor of Pennsylvania, and in foreign lands.

---

# PENNSYLVANIA COLONIZATION SOCIETY.

*Incorporated* 1830.

No. 609 Walnut Street.

*President*, Rt. Rev. Alonzo Potter, D. D.　　*Secretary*, Robert B. Davidson.
*Treasurer*, William Coppinger.

The object of this society is to encourage free colored persons to migrate and become citizens of the Republic of Liberia in Africa.

## THE PENNSYLVANIA SOCIETY FOR PROMOTING THE ABOLITION OF SLAVERY, AND FOR THE RELIEF OF FREE NEGROES UNLAWFULLY HELD IN BONDAGE, AND FOR IMPROVING THE CONDITION OF THE AFRICAN RACE.

*Incorporated by the Legislature of Pennsylvania, 1787.*

*President,* Dillwyn Parrish.                    *Treasurer,* Caleb Clothier.
*Secretaries,* Edward Lewis, T. E. Chapman.

Committees, who act in the recess of the Society, are appointed to carry out the several objects embraced in its title.

A fund is annually appropriated for the education and elevation of the free people of color in this city, and an evening school is kept up through the winter for persons of both sexes.

---

## THE HOME MISSIONARY SOCIETY OF THE CITY OF PHILADELPHIA.

*Organized in* 1835.        *Incorporated June* 7, 1845.

Office, North Street near 6th.

*President,* George H. Stuart.                    *Secretary,* R. K. Hoeflich.
*Treasurer,* Thomas T. Mason

Its object is twofold, "The spread of the Gospel and the relief of the poor." The first is sought by the distribution of Bibles and tracts and religious conversations amongst the poor. The second, by affording temporary relief, procuring employment for those able to work, and obtaining homes for destitute children, in town or country; preferring the latter, as they would thus be removed from bad influences, by which they may happen to be surrounded in the city.

## YOUNG MEN'S CHRISTIAN ASSOCIATION OF PHILADELPHIA.

*Instituted, June,* 1854.   *Incorporated, May,* 1857.

*President,* George H. Stuart.   *Corresponding Secretary,* John Wanamaker.
*Treasurer,* Wm. G. Crowell.

This Association is composed of members of various Christian denominations, Episcopalians, Baptists, Presbyterians, Methodists, Lutherans, &c., &c., who are associated for the improvement of the spiritual, mental and social condition of young men.

The means employed for the attainment of this object are devotional meetings, lectures, lyceum, a library for reference and circulation, reading-rooms, and committees to seek out young men taking up their residences in Philadelphia, and procure for them suitable boarding-houses and employment, and surround them with Christian influences.

## THE ASSOCIATION FOR THE CARE OF COLORED ORPHANS.

*Incorporated* 1829.

13th above Callowhill Street.

*Secretary,* Deborah M. Williamson.   *Treasurer,* Elizabeth North.

The object of this asylum is to receive children between the age of eighteen months and eight years into the *Shelter of Colored Orphans,* and at a suitable age to indenture them to persons in the country.

## THE HOME FOR DESTITUTE COLORED CHILDREN.

*Incorporated April* 11, 1856.

Girard Avenue near the Girard College.

*President,* Anna D. Morrison.   *Secretary,* Eliza Fell.
*Treasurer,* Susan M. Parrish.

Object similar to the Northern Home for Friendless Children.

## HOME FOR THE MORAL REFORM OF DESTITUTE COLORED CHILDREN.

*Not Incorporated.*

No. 708 Lombard Street.

*Secretary*, Deborah M. Williamson.　　　　　*Treasurer*, Sarah W. Cope.

In this institution the most destitute colored children are received and trained for usefulness. In addition to the home for these, there is a school for other poor children, under the care of the association, in the same building.

---

## THE PHILADELPHIA ASSOCIATION OF FRIENDS FOR THE INSTRUCTION OF POOR CHILDREN.

*Incorporated December 15, 1808.*

Situated in Winslow, (late Wager,) Street, between Race and Vine and Twelfth and Thirteenth Streets.

*Treasurer*, Richard Richardson.　　　　　*Clerk*, Edward Richie.

This charitable Institution has two schools of about one hundred and fifty colored children each, and is supported by voluntary contributions.

---

## INSTITUTE FOR COLORED YOUTH.

*Incorporated June 23, 1842.*

*Secretary*, M. C. Cope.　　　　　*Treasurer*, Edward Sharpless.

In this institution are taught the higher branches of an English education and the Latin language, with the view of qualifying colored youth of both sexes for teachers. There are also preparatory schools for boys and girls.

# Soup Houses.

## PHILADELPHIA SOCIETY FOR SUPPLYING THE POOR WITH SOUP.

### *Incorporated* 1841.

Green's Court, between Spruce and Pine Streets.

*President*, J. T. Bunting.        *Secretary*, J. J. Thompson.

*Treasurer*, Jeremiah Hacker.

This and the following six Soup Societies distribute bread and soup to the poor gratuitously during the winter months.

## THE WESTERN SOUP-HOUSE SOCIETY.

### *Not Incorporated.*

Corner of 17th and George Street.

*Secretary*, Samuel L. Baily.        *Treasurer*, George Vaux.

This Society was formed in November, 1837, with the late Charles Pierce as its President. Its object being to supply the poor of the southwestern part of the city with soup during the winter months. The annual expenses are between $2000 and $3000, to defray which it is dependent principally upon annual subscriptions.

## THE SPRING GARDEN SOUP SOCIETY.

### *Incorporated April 21, 1852.*

North side of Buttonwood Street, between 13th and Broad.

*President*, James Peters.        *Secretary*, F. Shoemaker.

*Treasurer*, J. H. Dohnert.

Gratuitous distribution of bread and soup. Open daily, except Sundays, from 11 A. M. to 1 P. M.

# NORTHERN SOUP SOCIETY OF PHILADELPHIA, FOR THE GRATUITOUS DISTRIBUTION OF SOUP TO THE POOR.

*Established*, 1817.   *Incorporated January* 17, 1839.

N. E. corner of 4th and Peters Street, above Brown.

*President*, Charles J. Sutter.                    *Secretary*, Samuel T. Childs.
*Treasurer*, T. Morris Perot.


# MOYAMENSING SOUP SOCIETY.

*Incorporated* 1835.

N. W. corner of 8th and Marriott Streets.

*President*, Charles Rhoads.                    *Secretary*, James M. Gibson.
*Treasurer*, Robert Graffen.


# SOUTHWARK SOUP SOCIETY.

*Incorporated February* 24, 1859.

Sutherland below Queen Street.

*President*, Robert Clark.       ·          *Secretary*, Edward S. Hall·
*Treasurer*, Benjamin Morton.


# KENSINGTON SOUP SOCIETY.

*Incorporated April* 18, 1853.

No       Shackamaxon Street.

*President*, Abraham P. Eyre.                    *Secretary*, J. K. Vaughan.
*Treasurer*, G. J. Hamilton.

# National Institutions.

## AMERICAN BIBLE SOCIETY.

*Incorporated* 1816.

Located at the City of New York.

---

## AMERICAN TRACT SOCIETY.

*Incorporated by the State of New York, May,* 1841.

*President,* Thomas S. Williams.     *Secretary,* William A. Hallock.

*Treasurer,* Moses Allen.

At the City of New York.

Pennsylvania Branch, at 929 Chestnut Street, Philadelphia.

---

## AMERICAN SUNDAY-SCHOOL UNION.

*Incorporated.*

No. 1122 Chestnut Street, Philadelphia.

*President,* Hon. John McLean.     *Secretary,* Frederick A. Packard.

*Treasurer,* W. J. Cheyney.

Objects.—As members of various Christian denominations, Baptist, Presbyterian, Methodist, Episcopalian, Reformed Dutch, Congregationalist, Lutheran, &c., we are associated for the purpose of establishing Sunday-schools in destitute parts of the country, supplying them with needful books, and aiding in the improvement of Sunday-schools generally.

Our organization contemplates one grand specific object,— viz., the gathering of untaught children into schools of religious instruction on the Lord's day. This is done by the labors of stated missionaries, whose office it is to explore new and recently-settled districts and neglected neighborhoods, and occasiona-missionaries, (chiefly college and seminary students,) organizing or encouraging schools, and supplying the needy with books.

3

# INDEX.

PAGE.

Forms of Devise and Bequest........................................................ 3

Introduction ................................................................................. 4

The Howard Institution................................................................. 5

The Pennsylvania Hospital........................................................... 6

The Protestant Episcopal Hospital............................................... 6

Charity Hospital ......................................................................... 6

Wills' Hospital............................................................................. 7

St. Joseph's Hospital.................................................................... 7

Children's Hospital...................................................................... 8

Female Medical College.............................................................. 8

Howard Hospital and Infirmary of Incurables............................. 8

Northern Home for Friendless Children....................................... 9

Union School and Children's Home............................................. 9

The House of Refuge.................................................................... 10

The Western Provident Society and Children's Home.................. 10

Union Temporary Home for Children.......................................... 10

Foster Home Association.............................................................. 11

Temporary Home Association...................................................... 11

Newsboys' Aid Society................................................................. 12

Lying-in Charity and Nurses' Society.......................................... 12

The Preston Retreat..................................................................... 13

Union Benevolent Association...................................................... 13

The Provident Society for Employing the Poor............................ 14

Female Society for the Relief and Employment of the Poor......... 14

Western Association for the Relief and Employment of the Poor...... 15

Northern Association for the Relief and Employment of Poor Women 15

35

The Central Employment Association........................................ 15
Philadelphia Society for the Employment and Instruction of the Poor 16
Pennsylvania Institution for the Deaf and Dumb....................... 16
Asylum for the Relief of Persons deprived of the use of their Reason. 17
Pennsylvania Institution for the Instruction of the Blind............ 17
Pennsylvania Training School for Feeble-minded Children.......... 18
The Orphans' Society of Philadelphia.................................... 18
Philadelphia Association for the Relief of Disabled Firemen........ 18
Indigent Widows and Single Women's Asylum.......................... 19
Penn Asylum for Indigent Widows and Single Women................ 19
The Grandom Institution.................................................... 19
The Apprentices' Library Company........................................ 20
The Young Men's Institute................................................. 20
The Spring Garden Institute............................................... 21
The Mechanic's Institute of Southwark.................................. 21
The Moyamensing Literary Institute..................................... 21
The Philadelphia City Institute........................................... 22
The West Philadelphia Institute.......................................... 22
The Wagner Free Institute................................................. 22
Pennsylvania Institute of Design......................................... 23
Philadelphia School of Design for Women............................... 23
Industrial Home for Girls.................................................. 23
Philadelphia Society for the Support of Charity Schools............ 24
Infant School Society of Philadelphia.................................. 24
Magdalen Society........................................................... 24
Rosine Association.......................................................... 25
Fuel Savings Society of Philadelphia.................................... 25
Philadelphia Dispensary.................................................... 26
Northern Dispensary of Philadelphia.................................... 26
The Homœopathic Medical College....................................... 26
Philadelphia Society for Alleviating the Miseries of Public Prisons.... 27
Pennsylvania Bible Society................................................ 27
Pennsylvania Colonization Society....................................... 27
Pennsylvania Society for promoting the abolition of Slavery......... 28
The Home Missionary Society.............................................. 28
Young Men's Christian Association....................................... 29

PAGE.

Association for the care of Colored Orphans.................................. 29

Home for Destitute Colored Children............................. 29

Home for the Moral Reform of Destitute Colored Children.............. 30

Institute for Colored Youth..................................... 30

Association of Friends for the Instruction of Poor Children............ 30

Philadelphia Society for Supplying the Poor with Soup.................. 31

Western Soup Society.............................................. 31

Spring Garden Soup Society........................................ 31

Northern Soup Society............................................. 32

Moyamensing Soup Society.......................................... 32

Southwark Soup Society............................................ 32

Kensington Soup Society........................................... 32

American Bible Society............................................ 33

American Tract Society............................................ 33

American Sunday-school Union ................................. 33